MW00911139

# COOKIES

Written and photographed by William Jaspersohn

MACMILLAN PUBLISHING COMPANY     NEW YORK

MAXWELL MACMILLAN CANADA     TORONTO

MAXWELL MACMILLAN INTERNATIONAL     NEW YORK   OXFORD   SINGAPORE   SYDNEY

Macmillan Publishing Company is part of the Maxwell Communication Group
of Companies. Macmillan Publishing Company, 866 Third Avenue, New York,
NY 10022. Maxwell Macmillan Canada, Inc., 1200 Eglinton Avenue East,
Suite 200, Don Mills, Ontario M3C 3N1
First edition.
Printed in the United States of America.

10  9  8  7  6  5  4  3  2  1

The text of this book is set in 13 point ITC Cheltenham Light.
The illustrations are black-and-white photographs reproduced in halftone.
Book design by Constance Ftera.

Library of Congress Cataloging-in-Publication Data
Jaspersohn, William.   Cookies : written and photographed by William
Jaspersohn. — 1st ed.     p.     cm.   Summary: A behind-the-scenes look at
how chocolate chip cookies are made at a Famous Amos cookie factory. ISBN
0-02-747822-X 1. Famous Amos Chocolate Chip Cookie Corporation—Juvenile
literature.   2. Cookie industry—United States—Juvenile literature.
3. Chocolate chip cookies—Juvenile literature.   [1. Famous Amos Chocolate
Chip Cookie Corporation.   2. Cookie industry.   3. Chocolate chip cookies.]
I. Title.     HD9058.C652U65  1993     664'.7525—dc20     91-45023

For Lucas, Anna, and Alexander Schulz—cookie eaters all!

Everybody loves cookies. In the United States, Americans gobble commercially made cookies at a rate of 6.5 million pounds a day, 2.4 *billion* pounds a year. That's about one pound of cookies a month or twelve pounds of cookies a year for every man, woman, and child in America. What's more, creating those cookies uses up some six hundred million pounds of flour, six hundred million pounds of sugar, and forty million gallons of eggs every year.

By the bag or by the box, cookies make their companies big money—about $3.5 billion annually.

Wally Amos was born in 1936 in a small house near the railroad tracks in Tallahassee, Florida.

As a boy growing up in New York City, Wally loved the chocolate chip cookies his Aunt Della used to bake. He baked them for himself when he got older. He discovered that people who tried the cookies always liked them. "I gave them as presents, and they always made people smile," he says. In 1975 he decided to go into business for himself, baking and selling the confection that came to be known as the Famous Amos Chocolate Chip Cookie.

On March 10, 1975, Wally opened the Famous Amos Chocolate Chip Cookie Store on Sunset Boulevard in Hollywood. It was the first store in the United States to sell nothing but chocolate chip cookies.

People loved the cookies, and the store did well. Before long, Wally opened more shops in other cities and they did well, too. By 1980 Wally found himself the president of a company with fifty cookie stores nationwide. Then, in 1988, Wally sold his company to a private investment group based in San Francisco. With his profits from the sale he settled in Hawaii, where he'd always wanted to live. He felt blessed with good fortune—and all because of the chocolate chip cookies his Aunt Della had taught him to bake.

Today, Famous Amos Chocolate Chip Cookies are sold through over 200,000 different food stores nationwide. The cookies are baked in several Famous Amos bakeries throughout the country, including this one in Augusta, Georgia.

Throughout the day and into the night, big trailer trucks loaded to the top with fresh ingredients roll up to the plant. When Wally Amos started his business, he decided that no artificial ingredients or preservatives of any kind would go into his chocolate chip cookies—only fresh flour, brown and white sugar, margarine, eggs, baking soda, vanilla extract, and chocolate chips. The company soon started making other kinds of cookies, always using only fresh ingredients: pecans, macadamia nuts, coconut, peanut butter, and raisins.

The basic ingredient of any cookie is flour, and the Famous Amos company buys its supply from mills like this one in Los Angeles.

The mill receives wheat for making its flour in big railroad hopper cars that roll into the mill yard practically every day. Workers open the cars' lower doors, and the wheat—from California, Montana, Texas, and Kansas—pours into ground-level holding bins.

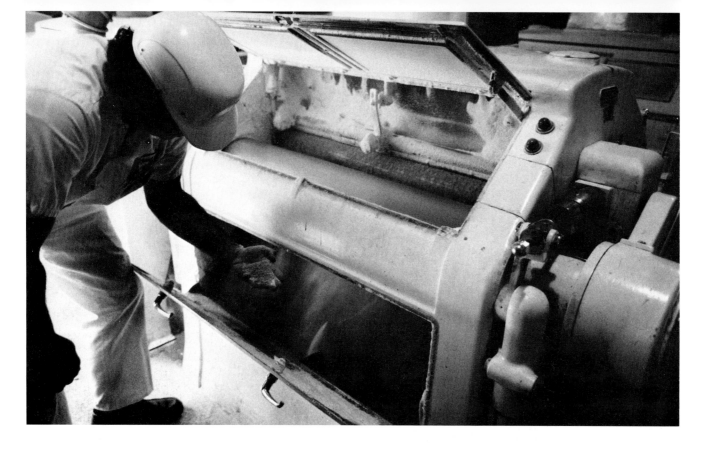

After the wheat is run on conveyers through a system of screens and magnets to rid it of stones, seeds, cockleburs, sand, and metal scraps, it is sprinkled with water to toughen its outer coat (called the bran coat) and left to sit for eighteen to twenty hours in a place called a temper bin. The next day, milling machines, equipped with heavy steel rollers, grind the wheat ten or twelve times until it has become a powdery tan dust.

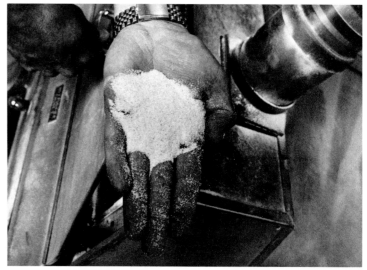

Between each grinding, the wheat dust is sifted through a system of screens housed in strange wooden boxes mounted on flexible legs. Electric motors shake each box and the screens separate the dust into different-sized particles. Tan and flakelike, the largest particles—called bran—are removed from the dust and later mixed with regular white flour to make bran flour. The medium-size white flour particles are ground again until they are the same size and texture as the smallest particles. And the smallest particles, from the innermost part of the wheat, are removed as finished white flour.

Once the flour has been sufficiently ground and sifted, it is either dumped into big bulk containers for shipping or bagged in heavy-duty paper sacks. Most mills sell their flour in different grades and mixtures. For its cookies, Famous Amos uses smooth, fine-textured pastry flour mixed with slightly coarser but better-binding all-purpose flour.

As the bags of flour come off the line, they are stacked on wooden forms called pallets until they are ready to be shipped. On average, Famous Amos uses over fifteen tons of flour a week in its cookies, so, to this mill, the company is a big and valued customer.

The chocolate chips that are such an
important ingredient of Famous Amos cookies
are made here, at the Ghirardelli Chocolate
Company in San Leandro, California.

The chocolate for the chips comes from fragrant beans called cocoa beans, which grow inside pods on wide-leafed tropical trees called cacao trees. Ghirardelli buys fifty-, sixty-, and seventy-kilogram (110-, 132-, 154-lb.) bags of the brownish dried beans from Ghana, Nigeria, the Ivory Coast, and Cameroon in West Africa; Samoa, New Guinea, and Malaysia in Asia and the Pacific; and Brazil, the Dominican Republic, and Ecuador in Latin America. The bags are stored in a warehouse until they are ready to be used.

To make chocolate chips, a worker starts by dumping bag after bag of cocoa beans into the hopper of a cleaning machine. Much like a wheat cleaner, the bean-cleaning machine uses sifting screens, a metal detector, and magnets to rid the load of metal and other debris. Ghirardelli wants its chocolate to be pure, so cleaning the beans is important.

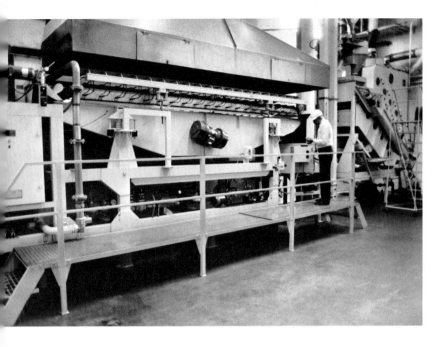

Once the beans have been cleaned, they are passed through a set of rollers that crack off the outer shells and break the beans into tiny pieces called nibs. A vacuum sucks away the shells and the nibs are roasted at 248 degrees Fahrenheit in huge, gas-fired ovens.

The nibs are rich in their own natural fat, known as cocoa butter.

The beans are now sucked through pipes to another room, where high-speed grinding machines pulverize them into a dark, thick liquid called chocolate liquor.

The chocolate liquor now undergoes a blending process where powdered beet sugar is added to sweeten it. The sugar also helps to dry and thicken the chocolate, so that it leaves the blending room in solid, rock-size chunks.

To improve the mixture's smoothness, the sweetened chocolate is ground yet again and then melted in gas-heated vats. More cocoa butter, along with vanilla, is mixed into it during the melting stage to further enhance the chocolate's taste.

When all the melting and mixing is done, the flavored chocolate is ready to be made into chips.

The chips are made this way: The chocolate is poured into a machine equipped with a specially perforated rack called a die. As the chocolate flows over the die, a press squeezes it through the die's two thousand nozzles. The die touches down on a conveyer belt. Presto! Left behind on the belt are two thousand chocolate chips! The chocolate continues to flow. The die touches down. Presto! Another two thousand chips appear as if from nowhere. The machine is a marvel of speed and efficiency. In a minute it can produce over 58,000 chips; in an hour, 3.5 million!

The warm chocolate chips are rapidly cooled to fifty degrees Fahrenheit in long cooling tunnels, then bagged for shipment to Famous Amos in Augusta. A single fifty-pound bag contains fifty thousand chips, enough for almost ten thousand chocolate chip cookies.

The flour, salt, sugar, and other dry ingredients that come to the Famous Amos bakery are stored on racks in the company's warehouse. Ingredients that need to be kept cool, such as eggs, margarine, and chocolate chips, are kept in small walk-in refrigerators.

Every weekday morning at eight o'clock workers begin laying out the ingredients for making Famous Amos Chocolate Chip Cookies.

They get everything ready in advance. Using electronic scales they measure out precise amounts of vanilla, baking soda, and salt so they can be added to the cookie dough the minute they are needed. Placing the bags and boxes of other ingredients on pallets near the mixing machines, they prepare to do this day's work: a million chocolate chip cookies with pecans.

Famous Amos mixes its cookie dough in two big mixers, each capable of stirring one thousand pounds of dough at a time. Using a special recipe on a formula card, the workers add the sugar, margarine, salt, baking soda, water, eggs, vanilla, flour, baking powder, pecans, and chocolate chips in the right quantities. By the time the workers have finished loading everything, the mixers are filled with fresh ingredients.

With the touch of two buttons, the mixer's metal door shuts tight, and an electric motor begins to turn the enormous, spiral-shaped beater within. The worker sets a timer on the control panel, which buzzes when the mixing is done.

Several minutes later, when the buzzer sounds, the door opens automatically and a worker inspects the dough. As always, it looks perfect—neither too sticky, nor too dry. It doesn't stick to the fingers when it is touched, and it's easy to shape into small balls.

Workers now remove the dough from the mixer. As one operates a button on the machine that causes the dough to be tipped forward, another uses a clean plastic shovel to scrape the dough into iron carts.

Mixed and ready, each cart of dough is wheeled to the baking line. There, a worker attaches a chain to the cart that lifts it into place over an automated machine called a depositor. It is the depositor that will actually shape the dough into cookies.

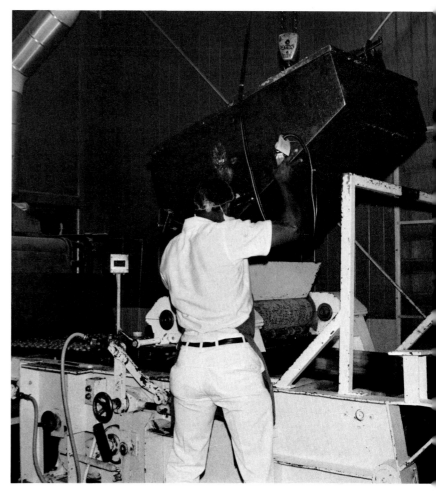

When the cart is in place, the worker opens its lower door and the dough drops into the depositor's topmost section, called the hopper. Two rotating drums inside the depositor pull the dough down to a Teflon strip called a die, which has cookie-width holes running along it. The dough passes through the holes, and a wire automatically cuts the dough into little disks. It is these disks that will soon become finished cookies.

Different-sized Teflon strips are available to cookie makers. Depending upon the number of holes in the strip, the depositor can cut as few as seven cookies at a time or as many as twenty. The strip used for cutting Famous Amos cookies contains fifteen holes, and the wire makes its cut across them once every second. That means that fifteen unbaked disks of dough fall onto the mesh-steel conveyer belt (called an oven band) every second. Nine hundred unbaked disks of dough fall onto the band every minute. And fifty-four *thousand* disks of dough fall onto the band every hour. By the end of one eight-hour shift this line will have produced some 432,000 cookies!

As the disks fall from the depositor to the oven band, a worker inspects them for flaws and separates any disks that might be stuck together. Inspecting the disks takes concentration. The oven band doesn't stop moving, and the depositor is continually being fed more dough.

Once the disks have been inspected, the oven band moves them into a double oven that is one hundred feet long. The oven is gas-fired and contains two separate heating zones. Depending upon the type of cookie, they can be moved slowly through the ovens and baked at low temperatures, or quickly, with the temperatures turned up high. Correct speeds and temperatures are important. If the cookies are baked too slowly, they'll dry out. If they're baked too quickly, the insides never get cooked.

Throughout the baking process, inspectors watch the progress of the cookies through small, lighted viewing windows. As the cookies bake, complex chemical reactions take place. The baking soda and baking powder in the cookies give off tiny bubbles of carbon dioxide gas as they are heated. The bubbles inflate the dough, making the cookies "stand up" as they're supposed to. Meanwhile, the heat breaks down the dough's sugars, making the dough sweeter. And the flour binds with the eggs, giving the cookies structure and texture.

When the cookies come out of the ovens a few minutes later, an inspector checks them for color, taste, and texture. Famous Amos Chocolate Chip Cookies are supposed to be crisp and crunchy, with a satisfying taste that stays on your tongue after you eat it. They should be round and blond, with lots of chocolate chips showing. No cookie should ever be too chewy or mushy.

These cookies are perfect—the dough has been correctly mixed and cut, the ovens have been heated to the proper temperature, the oven belt has been set at the proper speed.

As they pass out of the oven, the cookies move off the oven band onto a steel-mesh cooling belt. High-speed fans hidden under the belt cool the cookies quickly, while another inspector picks out and discards those cookies that are broken or have gotten stuck together in the baking process.

Once the cookies are cooled and inspected, a conveyer moves them to a machine called a separator, located one level above the bakery's main floor. The separator, with its system of chutes and buckets, can be adjusted to group the cookies by different amounts. For this batch of cookies à gauge on the separator has been set at one pound. That means that when a bucket below the chute system fills with one pound of cookies—no more, no less—it automatically tips forward, dumping the cookies into a second chute below it.

Each one-pound load of cookies is fed separately down a single pipe which deposits the load into its own brightly printed bag. The bags, mounted at the bottom of chutes on a motorized carousel, are placed there by workers who also watch to make sure that the separator functions properly.

Once filled with cookies, the bags are placed on a conveyer belt which runs through an automatic sealing machine. A heater in the machine warms the heat-sensitive glue along the top of the bag, and a pair of rollers squeezes the bag shut, sealing it. One by one, the finished sealed bags roll off the line at the rate of about fifty a minute.

At the end of the sealing line, the bagged cookies are either crated or boxed, and the crates and boxes are stacked for shipment on wooden pallets. To ensure that the crated cookies won't be damaged in shipment, a machine seals each palletload in plastic wrap.

Thus sealed and safely stacked, the cookies are gently driven by forklift to the company's warehouse, where they await shipment to stores throughout the country the next day.

The next morning, big, eighteen-wheeled trailer trucks arrive at the plant, and once again, the forklifts are on the move. Twenty-four pallets of cookies, some crated, some boxed, are loaded onto each truck, with each pallet holding about a hundred pounds of cookies. In all, a single truck will carry away over 300,000 cookies—enough to provide dessert and snacks to a small city.

This truckload of cookies is bound for a distributor three hundred miles north, in Virginia. The distributor, in turn, will sell the cookies to supermarkets throughout the mid-Atlantic states. Sales of the cookies to shoppers who buy them from the supermarkets provide profits to the store, distributor, trucking company—everyone—including the Famous Amos Company itself.

Starting any company requires a good idea, and Wally Amos's idea was a splendid one. It was simple, but who said great ideas have to be complicated? Wally's idea was: *Everybody loves cookies*. Judging from the response his cookies have gotten, he was right.

## Acknowledgments

The author wishes to thank Wally Amos and all the employees, past and present, of Famous Amos, who helped make this book possible. Special thanks to Mike Westhusing at Famous Amos; Suzanne Hammer, Ned Russell, and Matt Orlousky at Ghirardelli Chocolate; Blair Marvin, Jessica Marvin, Andrew Jaspersohn, and Sam Jaspersohn in Johnson, Vermont; Steve Geller and Karen Mankovich in Tempe, Arizona by way of Los Angeles; and Neal Porter, Harold Underdown, and Connie Ftera at Macmillan.